SESAME STREET

Baker, Baker, Cookie Maker

by Linda Hayward

illustrated by Tom Brannon

Random House 🏠 New York

Cookie Monster,
cookie eater,
mixes batter
with his beater,

drops the dough
onto the sheet,

bakes the cookies.
Good to eat!

He puts the cookies
on a plate,
takes a cookie . . .
Oops, too late!

Baker, baker,
cookie maker,
here comes a hungry
cookie taker!

COOKIES! COOKIES!

Monster treat.

Some for munchers,
some for crunchers,

13

none for the baker
on Sesame Street.

Cookie Monster,

cookie cutter,

makes a batch

with peanut butter,

cuts the cookies
out of dough,

18

puts them on the plate . . .

Oh, no!

Baker, baker,
cookie maker,
here comes another
cookie taker!

20

COOKIES! COOKIES!

Monster treat.

Some for hikers,
some for bikers,

none for the baker
on Sesame Street.

Cookie Monster,
cookie master,
makes more cookies
even faster.

He pats the cookies
nice and flat;
makes them,
bakes them.
Look at that!

Baker, baker,
cookie maker,
here come some *more*
cookie takers!

COOKIES! COOKIES!

Monster treat.

Some for hoppers,
some for moppers,

and *one* for the baker
on Sesame Street.

SESAME STREET®

Twinkle, Twinkle, Little Bug

by Katharine Ross
illustrated by Tom Brannon

Random House 🏠 New York

One night
Big Bird saw something
glowing in the dark.
"Look!" he said.
"A lightning bug!"

TWINKLE, TWINKLE, TWINKLE
went the lightning bug.

"Come here, little bug!
I won't hurt you,"
said Big Bird.
He put the lightning bug
in a jar.

TWINKLE, TWINKLE, TWINKLE

went the lightning bug.

"Ernie, look at my lightning bug," said Big Bird. "Twinkle for Ernie, little bug."

TWINKLE, TWINKLE, TWINKLE

went the lightning bug.

"Zoe, look at my
lightning bug,"
said Big Bird.
"Twinkle for Zoe,
little bug."

TWINKLE, TWINKLE, TWINKLE

went the lightning bug.

"Bert, look at my lightning bug," said Big Bird. "Twinkle for Bert, little bug."

But the lightning bug would not twinkle.

"Why won't you twinkle,
little bug?"
asked Big Bird.

"Maybe he's lonely,"
said Bert.

Big Bird talked to
the little bug
so he would not be lonely.

But the lightning bug
would not twinkle.

"Maybe he's tired,"
said Elmo.

Big Bird gave
the lightning bug
a pillow
so he could
take a nap.

But the lightning bug
would not twinkle.

"Maybe he's hungry,"
said Cookie Monster.

Big Bird gave the
lightning bug one of
Cookie Monster's
cookies to eat.

But the lightning bug
would not twinkle.

"Maybe he wants
to hear some music,"
said Hoots the Owl.

Hoots played some jazz.
Big Bird joined in.
"Twinkle, twinkle,
little bug!"
sang Big Bird.

But the lightning bug
still would not twinkle.

"Grover, why won't
my lightning bug twinkle?"
asked Big Bird.
"I talked to him.
I gave him a pillow
to sleep on.
I gave him a cookie to eat.
I played music for him.
I am his friend!"

"Would <u>you</u> twinkle
if you were
stuck in a jar?"
asked Grover.
"Gee," said Big Bird,
"I guess not."

Big Bird opened the jar
and set the little bug free.
"Twinkle, twinkle,
little bug!"
said Big Bird.

And the lightning bug did.

TWINKLE! TWINKLE! TWINKLE!